The Mermaid Secret

The Mermaid Secret

Vicki Blum

Cover by
**Laura Fernandez
& Rick Jacobson**

Illustrations by
Julie Rocheleau

Scholastic Canada Ltd.

Toronto New York London Auckland Sydney
Mexico City New Delhi Hong Kong Buenos Aires

Scholastic Canada Ltd.
175 Hillmount Road, Markham, Ontario L6C 1Z7, Canada

Scholastic Inc.
555 Broadway, New York, NY 10012, USA

Scholastic Australia Pty Limited
PO Box 579, Gosford, NSW 2250, Australia

Scholastic New Zealand Limited
Private Bag 94407, Greenmount, Auckland, New Zealand

Scholastic Ltd.
Villiers House, Clarendon Avenue, Leamington Spa,
Warwickshire CV32 5PR, UK

National Library of Canada Cataloguing in Publication

Blum, Vicki, 1955-
The mermaid secret / Vicki Blum ; illustrated by Julie Rocheleau.

ISBN 0-439-96916-6

I. Rocheleau, Julie II. Title.

PS8553.L86M47 2004   jC813'.54   C2004-900763-7

6 5 4 3 2 1   Printed in Canada   04 05 06 07 08

To my dear friend Sue

"...I take the wings of the morning,
and dwell in the uttermost parts of the sea..."
Psalms 139:9

Contents

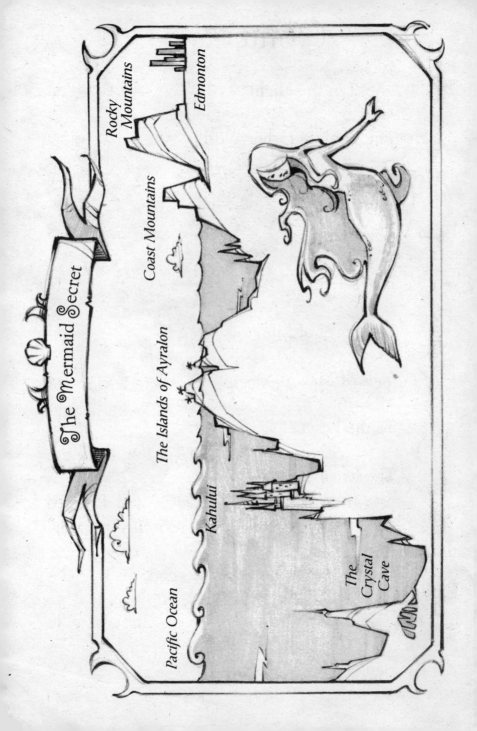

A Visit in the Night

My sister Kallie came into my room and stood beside my bed. I sat up and rubbed my eyes, still half asleep.

"I need you, Danya," she said. "The mermaids are in trouble and we have to save them."

I covered my face with my hands and flopped back down again. "Please don't do this to me," I moaned. "I'm sleeping."

"But this is important!" she pleaded.

I lay still with my eyes closed, hoping she'd go away. After a while I realized that wasn't going to happen so I sat back up again. "Everyone knows there's no such thing as a mermaid," I told her.

Kallie and I are as different as twins can be. She has blond hair and green eyes, but my hair and eyes are brown. And our looks are only the beginning.

Kallie's head is filled with dreams and her thoughts are in the clouds.

I'm much more down-to-earth, and my thoughts don't fly much higher than how to get paid for mowing the lawn.

Kallie believes in fairies and elves and pots of gold at the end of rainbows. I believe in getting my homework done on time.

Kallie makes wishes on falling stars. I just hope the meteor burns up before it hits Earth.

So you see, my sister and I don't have all that much in common. But in spite of our differences we care about each other a lot. So even though it was the middle of the night, I tried very hard to be patient.

"Even if mermaids really exist — which they don't — how do you know they're in trouble?" I asked, trying to pretend this was a sensible thing to talk about.

"One of them told me," Kallie explained. "She came into my bedroom a little while ago."

"All right then, why did she ask you for help and not someone else?"

"Because you and I are special to them," Kallie

said. "They know all about us. They know where we live."

I sighed in relief. This wasn't going to be so hard, after all. "You just had a very vivid dream," I said. "You'll hardly remember it in the morning."

She shook her head and frowned at me. "It wasn't a dream," she insisted.

"Then tell me something," I said. "How did the mermaid get all the way from the ocean to your room? Did she walk on her fins?" I didn't mean to be rude, but my patience was almost gone.

Kallie glared at me and said, "Don't be silly. Everyone knows that mermaids have magic. They can change their form to walk on land. But their magic doesn't work well on Earth and they can only stay here for a little while. That's why she didn't visit you, too. She had to hurry back."

"What was her name?" I asked.

"Brin," my sister answered without hesitation.

"How old was she?"

"A little older than us. It's kind of hard to tell with mermaids, though."

This was getting me nowhere fast. Kallie's imagination was just too good. By this time I was wide awake so I sat up again. Through my bedroom window I could see the stars glittering in the night sky

3

like a canopy of gems. Now that was real — and so beautiful that I never got tired of it. I got up to open the window and stuck my head outside for a better look.

"You don't believe me, do you?" Kallie said, coming up beside me.

I breathed in cool air, dampness, and the sweet scent of growing things. "Some things are real and some things aren't," I explained. I pulled my head in and closed the latch.

She nodded like she understood, but her green eyes glistened with tears. I saw her swallow, like something hurt her throat. I hated doing this to Kallie. Maybe I should just lie and tell her that I believed everything she said. But I was terrible at lying and she would see through it in a second.

I sighed. "It's late," I told her. "Let's go back to bed. We can talk about it in the morning."

She looked at me for a long moment and then nodded. "If that's what you want," she said, trying to sound like she didn't care. But as she turned away I saw her bite her lip to keep from crying. This wasn't a good way for things to end.

"Kallie —" I said, but the door had already clicked shut behind her.

After that I tried to sleep, but all I did was toss

and turn. My mind kept returning to Kallie's mermaids and I found myself wishing that my imagination was half as good as hers. It would be so handy when it came time to do that story for Language Arts. It was due in two weeks and I hadn't even started yet.

Miss McIntyre had told us three days ago that we had to write a story about some kind of mythical creature. I had no idea how to even begin. If Kallie was in my class she would have whipped up a dozen pages without even trying. But after tonight I could hardly ask her to help me. Things would probably be a bit uncomfortable between us for a while. I groaned, buried my face in my pillow, and tried not to think about it.

The next thing I knew I was waking up to sunlight on my face and the twitter of cheerful birds outside my window. I realized in dismay that I had slept in. I sat up and blinked my eyes. Something was bothering me but my brain was still too foggy to focus on the problem. I mulled it over for a minute. Oh yes. Kallie's mermaids.

I jumped out of bed and threw on my clothes. After washing my face and brushing my teeth in record time, I pounded downstairs and into the kitchen.

Most days I'm there ahead of my sister, but not today. It's another one of our differences. I'm an early riser, but she puts off getting up until the last possible moment. Morning is a calm, orderly time for me. Kallie blows about the house like a small hurricane, frantic that she has forgotten something important. Usually she has.

Kallie saw me coming through the doorway and bent her head to her cereal bowl. She didn't even look up when I sat down beside her. I smiled and pretended not to notice.

"Good morning, Mom," I said. "Good morning, Dad."

Mom smiled back and handed me the milk. Kallie stayed quiet and kept on chewing. Dad leaned over and kissed me on the cheek like he does every morning.

Dad is actually our stepfather, but I don't think of him that way. In my heart he's my father and always will be. He's large and strong, with a round face, ears that poke straight out from his half-bald head, and thick glasses that teeter on the end of his nose. But he would do anything for us and he makes my mother happy. He totally supports her becoming an artist. I'm going to marry someone just like him when I grow up.

"What's the matter?" he asked, looking from Kallie to me and back again. "I'm sensing some tension here."

"Nothing," my sister mumbled into her dish.

I dumped cereal into my bowl and sloshed on the milk. "We had a small disagreement," I said, sounding more cheerful than I felt. "But don't worry. We'll work it out."

Mom raised an elegant eyebrow. "I certainly hope so," she said, "because you'll be spending the evening together at Aunt Mattie's. Your father and I are going out on a date."

My spoon hit the table with a clatter. Oh, no. This was the worst possible time for us to visit Aunt Mattie. And if I tried to explain why, I knew they wouldn't understand.

Kallie looked up, her face brightening with pleasure. "That's wonderful!" she exclaimed. "We haven't seen Aunt Mattie for weeks!"

My day had just gone from bad to worse, and it was only eight-thirty in the morning.

The Book of Other Worlds

@unt Mattie is the kind of person that people turn around and stare at when she walks down the street.

Her hair is a black, frizzy ball and her fingernails are painted brighter than a sunset. She's short and plump, wears long black dresses, and is so weighed down with bracelets that she jingles. She works for a doctor, which means she has lots of white uniforms. In her closet all the black and white looks like penguins sleeping in a row. I told her once that she should give blue jeans and T-shirts a try. I even offered to take her shopping. She laughed so hard I thought she was going to choke.

Her house is even more peculiar than she is. It's small and dark, with jars lined up in rows on shelves and bundles of dried plants hanging from the ceiling. Every room you step into has a strange, new smell. She keeps a pet lizard and two snakes. I don't dare ask her what she feeds them.

And did I mention the cat? She talks to him like he's a real person. Rake is long and skinny and he scratches everything in sight. Aunt Mattie has never seemed to notice that parts of her sofa are shredded down to the bare wood.

°~°~°~°~°~°

Suddenly the lunch bell rang, jarring my mind back to the present. Books thumped on desktops. Papers rattled. Students all around me leaped to their feet. Miss McIntyre's voice rose above the clatter.

"Don't forget about your writing assignment," she reminded us. "Monday is a holiday, so let me know on Tuesday which mythological creature you have chosen. Remember, I want the outline handed in first."

I groaned as I elbowed my way toward the door. How did she come up with these crazy ideas, any-way? The kids in Kallie's class got to write a story about what they wanted to be when they grew up. It was just my luck to get a teacher who made everything harder than it should be.

During the afternoon my lack of sleep made it hard to stay awake. I dozed off twice during math, but luckily Taryn noticed my nodding head and poked me from behind. Later, during a spelling test, I closed my eyes for just a moment and when I opened them again the test was half over. I knew not to ask my teacher to start again. Miss McIntyre doesn't give second chances.

My day of misery ended at last. I threw my books into my backpack the instant the bell went off, and hurried down the hall. I had to find a book for the dreaded assignment before the school library closed.

"Where are the books on mythology?" I asked the librarian.

She peered at me from behind her computer screen and waved vaguely toward the shelves.

I had a pretty good idea where to find them anyway. I rushed over to where I thought they might be and lurched to a stop, my heart sinking. There wasn't a book in sight.

"Sorry, I forgot to tell you," the not-very-helpful librarian said. "They're all checked out."

It was a perfect ending to my dismal day. I left the school and trudged down the street that led to Aunt

Batty's (oops, Aunt Mattie's) house. Kallie was probably fifteen minutes ahead of me by now. I wasn't in a big rush to get there and face her again. Besides, the slower I walked, the less time I would have to spend talking about impossible things.

Though I had put it off as long as I could, I finally reached my aunt's house and dragged my feet up the front steps. As I reached out to ring the bell, the door creaked open in front of me.

Kallie and Aunt Mattie stood together, framed in the doorway. Aunt Mattie actually looked happy to see me. Her round, pink face beamed with joy. My sister's face was like the beginning of a spring thaw — still cool but starting to warm around the edges. I had to admit that I didn't blame her. If I had been in her place I would have been mad at me, too.

Aunt Mattie threw her arms around me. She's always been a very warm and caring person. I'm sure that's why all of the doctor's patients like her. But she's so much like Kallie that it makes me nervous. In fact she's more like Kallie than Kallie is. Aunt Mattie believes in mermaids, too. But she also believes in fairies and other worlds, and something called the Balance of Magic.

And that's not the only thing about her that's odd. She's so good at guessing what I'm thinking that it scares me. If I'm sad, and paste on a happy smile, she sees right through it. When I'm with her, I might as well forget about lying. I know she can't actually read minds, but sometimes it sure seems like it. Why can't I have normal relatives like all my friends do?

Aunt Mattie held me at arm's length and gazed fondly into my eyes. "My darling Danya," she said. "It's so good to see you! Are you hungry? I have clam chowder on the stove and cornbread cooling on the counter."

In spite of her odd ways, Aunt Mattie means well. She knows that Kallie and I both love seafood and she always tries to please us. But you never know what will end up in the pot. One time she threw in the whole fish. We picked sharp little spines out of our teeth for hours.

The chowder smelled wonderful, though. I hadn't realized how hungry I was. As we slurped and munched, I filled Aunt Mattie and Kallie in on everything that had happened that day. Kallie rolled her eyes about the school library. Aunt Mattie clicked her tongue in sympathy. She said she understood how hard it must be to get assignments done.

"I have an idea," she exclaimed suddenly, leaping from her chair. "We'll look in *my* library!"

I groaned to myself. Aunt Mattie's library isn't the usual kind where volumes are neatly stacked in order by author or subject. It's more like the result of a small avalanche. Books are piled in corners, scattered on tables, and spilling out of drawers and cupboards. They lie everywhere but on the shelves. You can't take a step without tripping. You can't reach for a book without three more crashing down on you. Finding the one you need is just about impossible.

"That's okay," I said, trying to sound cheerful. "But thanks, anyway."

"Don't be silly," she said with a wave of her hand. "It's not okay. Besides, I know exactly which book will help you the most."

"Oh?" said Kallie, looking interested. "What book do you mean?"

So that's how, a half-hour later, I came to be sitting in Aunt Mattie's library reading *The Book of Other Worlds,* written by someone with a name I couldn't pronounce.

The first thing I thought when I saw the book was that only Aunt Mattie would own anything so impractical. It was as big as a suitcase and so old I feared it would crumble to dust in our hands. The cover was brown and cracked. The pages were yellow and curled around the edges. It took all three of us to

hoist it onto the table.

Kallie dragged a chair across the floor and plopped down beside me. I lifted the dark leather cover. Its table of contents told us that the section about people came first. The names were listed in alphabetical order. Hardly any of them were familiar to me. I did recognize King Arthur and Merlin, and a couple of others. Then we came to the section that told us about places.

I skimmed as I flipped the pages. *Antillia...Atlantis...Avalon...Ayralon...*Kallie's hand came down on the paper with a thud. "Let's read about this one," she said, holding the book open at the place called Aryalon. "Do you mind?"

I nodded in agreement since she wasn't giving me any choice. I started to read.

Ayralon is an ocean world topped by a few small islands scattered along the equator. The merpeople who live there can breathe air as well as water, but they spend most of their time under the sea. Because Ayralon is so closely aligned with Earth, sometimes humans lost in storms cross over through one of the portals that join the two worlds. The Ayralonians are a kindly people and always return visitors home unharmed.

No one lives on the islands of Ayralon, though at times the merpeople will swim up from their underwater cities to bask in the sun. Ayralonians are tied to their world by magic, and the farther away they go from it, the weaker they become. Some say a race of sea nymphs with great magical powers lives far below, in the darkest depths of Ayralon's ocean world. This rumour has never been proven.

Kallie's eyes glowed with excitement as she read. I stared at her, my heart sinking to my shoes. Aunt Mattie's crazy old book was talking about these places like they actually existed. It was just feeding Kallie's mermaid delusion, making it stronger than ever. I tried to close the book but my sister held it open.

"Why don't you write a story about mermaids, Danya?" she said. "I could help you."

I just sat there, too upset to move. I didn't know what to say. If I told her yes, her fantasy would keep on growing. If I said no, I would hurt her again.

After a long, agonizing moment I managed to mumble, "Thanks, Kallie, but I haven't decided what to write about yet. I need more time to think it over."

The Spell

By Saturday morning things were nearly back to normal between Kallie and me, though I still hadn't decided what topic to choose for my story. Kallie hadn't brought up the subject of mermaids again, but I could tell it was still on her mind. It was still on both of our minds, hidden behind every glance, waiting in the silence between every word we spoke. So when she asked me to go swimming at the rec centre, I practically leaped from my chair. Now for a while I wouldn't have to worry about it.

We grabbed our bathing suits and headed for the door.

"Be back by noon," Mom called after us. "Don't forget that we're planting the garden this afternoon!"

How could we forget when she had reminded us three times? I could tell by the look on Kallie's face that she planned on making our swim a long one. She didn't like garden planting — or weeding — any more than I did.

We ended up turning our bike ride into a race. I held back a bit and let Kallie win, but of course I didn't tell her that. She's only happy about beating me if she can do it fair and square.

She glared at me as we changed into our bathing suits. "You let me win," she said. It wasn't a question.

I shrugged my shoulders and avoided her gaze. "What makes you think that?"

"You're trying to make up for hurting my feelings on Thursday night," she said. "I can always tell when you feel guilty about something. You don't need to, you know. I forgave you yesterday. Not first thing, but definitely later on."

I didn't answer because I wasn't ready to talk about it yet. I was already halfway out the door anyway. She scrambled after me, laughing and trying to grab my arm. "Get back here and admit it, you coward!" she cried.

That's more like it, I thought as we plunged into

the deep end of the pool. I like it so much better when we're friends.

Kallie followed me down. Both of us are excellent swimmers in spite of the fact that we never have much time to practise. We prefer lakes to pools because there's no chlorine in the water. Sylvan Lake is one of our favourite spots, but we only get the chance to go there once or twice a summer. We've never even seen the ocean. Dad keeps telling us he'll take us there some day, but it hasn't happened yet. When he mentions it, my mother stiffens and stops whatever she's doing. Then she starts making excuses, like we don't have enough money or the car might break down and leave us stranded. After a while Dad gives up trying to talk her into it and we put it off for another year.

Right now we had the pool all to ourselves. What a break. I rolled over and kicked. Kallie followed me up. Her face broke the surface close to mine. She grinned while the water glistened in her golden hair and dripped off the end of her nose.

"Come with me to Ayralon, Danya," she said, grabbing both of my wrists in her hands. I stiffened in surprise. Her grip was stronger than I realized. A chill ran through me, though the water was warm.

"Cut it out, Kallie," I said, kicking and trying to

yank free. "This isn't funny."

"It isn't meant to be," she replied.

I didn't like the sound of her voice. It was quiet and serious. And I didn't like the way her green eyes glittered as she looked at me.

"It isn't real," I said to her. "Not the people in Aunt Mattie's book, not Ayralon, and especially not the mermaids."

We hung there, treading water, locked together in a silent struggle of her will against mine.

"All right," she said at last. "I'm sorry, Danya, but you're giving me no choice. Brin told me how to do this, and I hope I get it right. She said that the portals are made in two ways. Sometimes they're formed by accident at sea, with wind and rain and lightning. The other way is to be in water — and say the magic words. Prepare yourself for a fast and furious ride."

Now I was starting to get really angry. I had no idea what she was talking about but whatever it was, I didn't like it. I opened my mouth to shout at her, to tell her she had no right to treat me this way and she should let me go this instant. But she spoke before I got the chance. Her strange words made me shiver, as though small, slithery things were crawling across my skin.

"Wind of sea and earth and fire,
Take me where I most desire.
Whirl me, twirl me, lift me high,
Return me softly as a sigh."

It all happened so quickly that there was no escape. The instant the chant ended, the water around us seemed to explode. I heard a loud slurping noise, followed by a crash. The water churned, gathering speed at a terrifying rate. It spun us in circles, faster and faster, until I could no longer see anything but bubbles and foam. I screamed at the same instant as Kallie let go of my wrists. I saw her fly past me, a tangle of arms and legs and long streaming hair. My screams gurgled to silence as my throat filled with water. I gagged, struggling for air.

It was over as suddenly as it had begun. Somehow I found the air I needed and breathed in, then broke into a fit of coughing. As my dizziness subsided, I saw with relief that Kallie was still swimming beside me.

Only we were no longer in the same pool. In fact, we weren't in a pool at all. We were floating in a warm, silent sea, not far from the shore of a beautiful tropical island. Though I had seen lots of travel ads

in magazines, nothing compared to this. It couldn't be real, of course. I squeezed my eyes shut, but when I opened them again, the island was still there.

Sunlight dazzled off a blue-green ocean that was as still and clear as glass. Fish as bright as bathtub toys darted past us, pausing only long enough to nibble at our toes. A stretch of silver sand lay only a few strokes away. I was dimly aware that Kallie had begun pulling me toward it. Beyond the sand a row of palm trees reached up toward a sky that sparkled like a giant sapphire bowl. Birds of every colour and variety soared overhead or perched among the palm leaves.

My feet touched bottom and then I felt Kallie drag me up onto the beach. My legs lacked the strength to do anything more than wobble uselessly beneath me. I took a couple of lopsided steps and fell onto the sand.

Kallie flopped down beside me. "Welcome to Ayralon," she said.

4

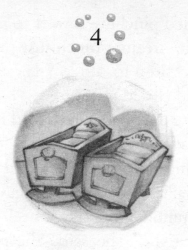

The Island

I'm not sure how long I lay there with my heart thudding in disbelief. Logic told me that none of this was real. But every time I closed my eyes and opened them again, the island was still there — and I realized it wasn't going to go away.

I've always been a great fan of science. It explains just about everything in life. But science couldn't explain how I had just been flung from a swimming pool on Earth into an ocean in another world.

Perhaps this was all a dream, triggered by Aunt Mattie's book. Or maybe I had almost drowned in the pool and this was the result of a lack of oxygen to the brain. I tried pinching myself to see if I was real — but you can dream a pinch just the same as anything else. Too tired to think, I lay my head on the warm sand and closed my eyes.

"Take all the time you need," said Kallie kindly. "I know this must be a terrible shock."

After a while I looked up. "I'm sorry I didn't believe you, Kallie," I said. I didn't have to work hard at sounding humble. I felt like a heel.

"That's all right," she said. She pushed a soggy string of hair from her eyes. "Your strong will is one of your best qualities. I knew what I was up against from the start." She paused, then added, "You turned out to be more stubborn than I thought, though."

I groaned into the sand. "Go ahead and make me feel bad," I said. "I deserve it."

She shook her head. "I'm not trying to. You feel bad enough already. Besides, who in their right mind would have believed me?"

"That's true," I admitted. I felt a little better.

For the next few minutes we just lay there in silence, catching our breaths. From our place on the beach I could see the sandy shore curving off in both directions around the bend. Colours were so bright here that I had to squint to keep my eyes from hurting. Even Kallie looked more alive, somehow. Her skin had a creamy glow and her green eyes sparkled in a way I'd never seen before. Glancing at my own arms, I could see that they were gleaming, too.

I patted the sand. "Is this one of the islands where the mermaids come to sun?" I asked. In spite of the valiant effort I was making, I nearly choked on the word "mermaid." I still had trouble with the idea, and I hadn't quite recovered from the shock of coming here. The wild pattering of my heart was only now beginning to slow. It had been a rough few minutes.

"Of course," Kallie replied. "The portal we came through always leads to this island, just as it will always take us home again. Brin told me that this island is close to where she lives. From this beach, we're supposed to face the water, then head left along the shore until we come to a garden. That's where she said she'd meet us."

"At least we don't have to worry about getting lost," I said, gazing around. "It's a small island. If we follow the shore for long enough, we'll end up back where we started."

We plunged back into the water to wash the sand off our bathing suits. Then we set out along the beach.

Neither one of us wore a watch, but it couldn't have been more than a few minutes later that we discovered Brin's garden. Kallie saw it first, and started inland toward a cluster of fruit trees snuggled up against a small hill. A stream that began somewhere in the larger hills beyond trickled downwards, tumbled over a rocky outcrop, and gurgled happily toward the sea. As we drew closer, I saw to my delight that a pool had formed at the base of the waterfall. Tropical flowers bloomed in abundance, circling the pool like a fragrant wreath.

A sudden screech of delight sent me rushing to Kallie's side. She stood knee-deep in the centre of a strawberry patch, staring at berries the size of golf balls. I bent, plucked one free, and popped it in my mouth. I had never tasted anything so delicious or so sweet.

"Look," Kallie said, and pointed. I saw bushes laden with blackberries and raspberries. Next to them, vegetables had been planted in straight, well-tended rows. Beyond was a grove of apricot, peach and cherry trees. A pathway wound through the trees, and I was curious about where it led. Perhaps we could see...

Kallie clearly felt the same way. She grinned, beckoned me to follow, and took off running. I grabbed

another strawberry and dashed after her.

The trail was smooth and well worn under our bare feet, though we had to duck to avoid overhanging branches. A minute later the orchard opened into a small meadow and we came to an abrupt halt, gasping in surprise.

In the centre of the meadow sat a cottage — so quaint and pretty that for a moment I thought of my mother's paintings. Flowers fluttered on both sides of a walkway that led to the wooden door. The cottage walls were stone, and straw was heaped on the rooftop. But the windows were shuttered, and no smoke rose from the one small chimney.

"Look at this!" cried Kallie, darting forward. Someone had painted miniature scenes on many of the larger stones that made up the walkway. On one, a merboy clung to the back of a dolphin as it soared high above the waves. The dolphin's grin was as wide as the boy's. On another, three young mermaids lay on a beach, basking in the sun. A third showed two mermaids diving into the sea while moonlight glistened on their sleek, silver bodies and turned their hair to cobwebs made of gold.

We followed the trail of pictures to the door of the cottage and stood there for a moment, wondering what to do next.

Kallie looked at me and shrugged. "We won't learn anything by standing here," she said, rapping on the door. She waited for a moment longer and then pushed it open. It moved soundlessly beneath her touch. She stepped through the opening. I glanced nervously over my shoulder, then followed her inside.

The room was bare except for a table, four chairs, and a couch. Against one wall stood a stone fireplace, still grey with the ashes of a fire long grown cold. A fine layer of dust lay over everything. Leaving a trail of footprints behind us, we stepped into the other room.

It was a bedroom, furnished with a wooden bed and night table.

"This looks like a guest house," Kallie said, echoing my own thoughts. "Maybe visitors from Earth stay here."

I looked around. "Then there must be an outhouse," I said.

Kallie rolled her eyes, then peered behind the bed.

"Come look at this!" she cried. Two tiny cradles lay on the floor beneath the window.

Neither one of us knew what to say. Mermaids would have little use for cradles, which meant these must have been made for human visitors. Perhaps an entire family had been pulled through the portal and stayed here for a while. We studied them for a moment, wondering what to make of it.

That's when we heard the patter of feet from the other room.

"Brin?" said Kallie.

We barely had time to turn and a girl burst through the open doorway.

When she saw us she skidded to a halt. She stood and stared, trying to catch her breath.

I couldn't take my eyes off her, so astonished was I at her appearance. She was the most beautiful creature I had ever seen. The mermaid paintings on the walkway couldn't do her justice.

Brin had come to us in human form. Still damp with seawater, her blue-green legs gleamed with silver highlights, glistening as though sprinkled with diamond dust. Her bathing suit was woven from strands of seaweed, and her wet hair rippled down her back like golden ropes.

"Brin!" Kallie cried. The smile Brin gave her in return could have lit up a city.

"You came!" she exclaimed, taking Kallie's hand. "And you brought Danya with you. I've been waiting and hoping. I'm so glad you're here!"

"How can we help you?" Kallie asked.

"Come to the city of Kahului with me. Crispus, my chief advisor, will explain everything."

"City?" I asked. "Advisor?"

"Of course," said Kallie. "We'll go right now." For her, the mystery of the cottage and the cradles was already forgotten. But my mind was still buzzing with questions that needed to be answered.

I trailed behind them as they headed for the door. "Who built this cottage?" I said. "What are the cradles for?"

Brin laughed. It was a delightful sound — like bubbles bursting in air. "Which shall I answer first?" she teased. "I might as well tell you now. You'll find out soon enough, anyway. The cradles belonged to the two of you. This cottage is the place where you were born."

5

Brin's Tale

"Born?" Kallie cried. "Did our mother live here?" Her voice shrilled with excitement. I could tell by the look on her face that her imagination had taken hold of the idea and was running wild.

There was no way I would ever be convinced. It was hard enough to accept the fact that I was actually in Ayralon. How could I ever believe that I was born here?

Besides, I had proof that Mom had never lived here. She hated the ocean. She had always hated the ocean. At home she wouldn't take us there, even when we begged and pleaded.

But my logical mind (always my worst enemy) kept right on going.

Why does she hate the sea? I asked myself. She's never given you a reason. Maybe she did live here once, with your father, and something bad happened. Maybe she doesn't ever want to see the ocean again because it brings back all those unhappy memories.

I groaned to myself as I followed Brin and Kallie back along the path to the garden. I didn't need them to convince me. I had almost convinced myself.

"Yes, your mother did live here," Brin replied. "She was brought here during a thunderstorm and met your father. He was one of us. His name was Leron."

I shook my head in protest, but neither one of them noticed.

Kallie skipped with delight. "I thought so!" she exclaimed. "I mean...I didn't think it...exactly. But I knew there was something different about Danya and me. I've always known!"

"I don't think there's anything different about us," I said. "We're really quite ordinary." But they weren't listening.

"Tell us more about our father," Kallie pleaded.

It was true that our mother hardly ever talked about our real father. About all she had ever said was that he had died before we were born, and that he came from somewhere far away. She had never told us where, even when we asked.

Brin and Kallie continued to talk as they made their way toward the beach.

"Your father built the cottage for your mother and lived with her here," Brin said. "She couldn't live in our underwater city, of course. Our magic is strong, but it can't turn humans into mermaids. I never met your parents, but Crispus told me all about them. Your mother was the first and only human ever to live in Ayralon. Your parents were special, and very courageous. We've been told that your father loved your mother very much."

I swallowed the lump in my throat. It hurt all the way down.

"But we already have a father," I objected, thinking of Dad — the only father I had ever known. "And he loves her, too. He loves all of us." I paused, then added: "He's been to every one of my Christmas concerts since kindergarten."

Brin halted at the water's edge. I tried not to stare as her feet began to glitter with tiny pinpoints of light.

"I realize your stepfather loves you," she said kindly. "But this isn't about him. This is about you and Kallie saving my people from a terrible danger."

"We understand," said Kallie. "We'll do whatever you ask."

The pinpoints of light were already up to Brin's knees. The only thing was, she no longer had any knees.

"I need you come to my city and meet my advisors," said Brin. "They'll explain everything."

Brin was turning into a fish right in front of us. And she wanted Kallie and me to follow her down to her city under the ocean and she expected us to believe that we were half-mermaid. What if she was making a mistake? What if the magic wouldn't work for us and we couldn't breathe? Could she keep us from drowning?

Brin slid into the water because by this time she no longer had any legs to stand on. The pinpoints of light had disappeared, leaving behind the slender, gleaming tail and graceful fin of a true mermaid. She was lovely.

"Will we change into real mermaids, too?" Kallie asked, her eyes like stars.

"I don't know," replied Brin as the water lapped around her silky, shimmering form. "You girls are the only mer-humans ever born in Ayralon. You're the first of your kind. But don't worry — you can breathe under water. That's already certain, because you could when you were young. It used to worry your mother. When your father died, she took you back to Earth so she wouldn't lose you to the sea."

That sounded so much like my mother that I almost let myself believe what Brin was saying.

"But I choke on water all the time," I pointed out.

"You choke because you try to keep the water out," Brin explained. "You can't breathe unless you let it into your lungs as we do."

"I'm not afraid to try!" Kallie cried, and she hurtled past me, plunging headfirst into the water. I stared in horror at the spot where she disappeared beneath the waves, my heart banging. I waited and waited, but she didn't surface. Brin moved out a little further from shore, then turned to look at me with large, troubled eyes.

"You have to trust me," she said.

I licked my lips, but my mouth was so dry with fear that it didn't help.

"Think about it," she reasoned. "Who painted those pictures on the stones? Didn't they look familiar?"

"Yes," I admitted. "They looked like my mother's paintings. But in all these years, she never said anything to us about Ayralon. Why didn't she tell us the truth about where we came from?"

The tip of Brin's emerald and sapphire tail shimmered in the sunlight. I could hardly drag my eyes away. "It's not your mother's fault," she said. "My people erased most of her memories of Ayralon when she left. She only remembers the important things — like your father and the day that you were born. I was told she wanted it that way."

Brin held out her hand to me.

I gazed into the sea and caught a glimpse of Kallie's red bathing suit and yellow hair streaming past. It was obvious that my sister was still very much alive — and having a great time.

Maybe it was true, then. Maybe our father had been a merman, just like they said. Kallie did look a lot like Brin. But I didn't look like them at all. I looked like my totally human mother, which meant that Kallie might have all the mermaid genes. Maybe the magic of Ayralon worked for her but not for me...

"Please trust me," Brin said again, almost pleading now. "I won't let you drown. If you can't breathe, I'll let you go."

I don't know why I finally decided to give her a chance. Perhaps I knew deep down that she would never let me come to any harm. Something about her

made me want to trust her. My stomach lurched sickly as I waded into the water and took her hand. Then I let her pull me further into the sea.

The thrust of her tail was so powerful that within seconds we were too far out for me to touch bottom. Down we plunged, into the azure depths, deeper and deeper. I held my breath and tried not to think about how far up I would have to go for air. Then Brin stopped and spiralled toward me, a frown creasing her lovely brow.

°You've got to try, Danya,° she said. °You can't hold your breath forever.°

There was no way I could make myself breathe under water. Every instinct I had screamed against the thought. How had Kallie done it?

°It's going to be all right, Danya,° Brin assured me.

I shook my head and pulled free. I was nearly out of air. As I drew up my legs to kick to the surface, a school of tiny fish darted past my nose. I was so surprised that I opened my mouth and sucked in water — sweet water, fresh as a waft of mountain air.

Then I breathed some more. It felt like the most wonderful thing I had ever done. Brin threw up her arms in wild joy. She grabbed me by the waist and spun me up and over her head in a huge, dizzy circle.

The school of fish scooted away.

°I knew you could do it, Danya!° she cried. And she hugged me so hard that I almost lost my new-found breath.

The Jewel of Life

Before long we had caught up with Kallie. When she saw that I was breathing she grinned and gave me a thumbs-up. I grinned happily back at her.

"It's not very far down to our mercity," Brin explained as we swam. "We're not deep-sea creatures as some of your people believe. We need warmth and sunlight to survive. But when we're hunting for food, we often go much deeper."

"What do you eat?" I asked.

"Many kinds of fish and other sea creatures. We use merfire to cook them — it burns underwater. We also eat a lot of seaweed, plus the fruits and vegetables that we grow on the islands. Those we eat raw.°

°It sounds really healthy,° I mused. °Raw fruit and vegetables, lots of fish...and no burgers and fries!°

°Burgersinfrize?° Brin said, looking puzzled. °What's burgersinfrize?°

Up to that point I hadn't realized how much I took my own way of life for granted. Two of my favourite foods — ice cream and pepperoni pizza — simply didn't exist in this world. And even if they did, they could never be eaten under water.

°Ground up meat...° I started to explain. Then I caught sight of the mercity and halted in mid-sentence, speechless with awe.

The merfolk had carved their city out of crystal and gold.

It rose from the ocean floor all glittery and bright, with towers and spires that peaked above the surrounding rocks and scattered sunlight like a prism. As we drifted closer I saw that the buildings were made of stone as smooth and fine as polished marble, dark gray to gleaming white. Light shimmered down from the surface, setting ablaze the gold-trimmed windows and the inlaid mother-of-pearl that decorated the doors. Streets were wide and bright, teeming with fish, plants and coral of every colour in the rainbow.

°I've never seen anything so beautiful,° I marvelled. I pointed at a nearby window. °In our world, gold is melted into bricks and locked up.°

Brin chuckled. °Visitors are stunned to see how much gold we have. I'm sure they all wish they could take some home. But not everyone stops with wishes... and recently something dreadful happened. That's why I need you to meet with my advisors.° She sounded worried.

°I guess you don't use money here,° said Kallie.

°We know about money,° Brin responded, °but you're right, we don't use it. We trade for what we want, or simply give when there's a need. There's plenty here for everyone.°

°I wish our world would work like that,° I muttered.

By this time we had reached the heart of the city. As Brin led us on a winding course between the buildings, I couldn't help but notice the attention we were drawing from the merfolk. Mermaids peeked out through the windows of their homes as we floated by. Mermen stopped their work and glanced our way. Merchildren playing water tag paused and stared with wide, puzzled eyes.

°Please excuse my people,° Brin apologized. °They've never seen humans breathe under water

before. Everyone's very curious, and I'm afraid they're not good at hiding it.°

°We don't mind,° Kallie assured her, waving cheerfully at a group of gawking merboys. They stared back at her in shock, then scattered like frightened fish.

Brin paused in front of the most elaborate doorway we had yet seen, pulled it open, and beckoned for us to follow her inside. Marble columns led down a hallway draped with woven seaweed tapestries that fluttered in the gently moving currents. Lamps in gold brackets gleamed above our heads. I could only assume that they were powered by magic, for there was no electricity here. Schools of red and blue fish swirled about our faces, then scurried away.

The room at the end of the passageway was as fine and stately as that found in any human palace. Paintings of regal-looking merpeople adorned the walls. Gold statues gleamed in corners. Mermaids drifted in small groups, talking quietly or merely waiting. In the centre of the room a circle of chairs hung suspended from the ceiling like swings. One of the mermen seated there loosened the tendrils of seaweed that held him in place and swam forward to meet us. He wore a crimson cape fastened with a seashell clasp. His hair was the colour of fire, and his tail — as thick and muscled as a dolphin's — gleamed with orange highlights. He was a magnificent creature.

The merman greeted us with a polite nod, then bowed to Brin.

°Welcome back, Keeper,° he said.

I turned to Brin. °Why did he call you that?° I asked, puzzled.

°Because I'm the Keeper of the Jewel,° she explained, °and the Ruler of Ayralon.°

°Cool!° Kallie exclaimed. I stared at Brin, not knowing what to say. The problem must be a serious one for the merpeople to have sent the ruler of their world to find us.

°What do Keepers do?° I said, hoping it wasn't impolite to ask.

°I watch over the Jewel of Life,° explained Brin. °It's my job to make sure it's kept safe and that the magic is preserved.° With those words, a look of profound sadness flickered across her face.

°Thank you for coming,° the shining man in front of us said. °I am Crispus, Chief Advisor to the Keeper.° He nodded at an older mermaid beside him. °I'd like you to meet Alora. She is also an advisor. We welcome you to Kahului, the capital city of Ayralon. So you are Leron's children! I knew you when you were babies. I'm pleased to see that you've grown into fine young ladies.°

°We're happy to meet you — again,° Kallie said.

I nodded, not feeling quite as happy.

°Come sit with us,° Crispus said, gliding over to the hanging chairs. When we were settled on our seaweed seats, he began to speak.

°The Keeper of the Jewel has brought you here for a reason,° he said. He leaned forward and pinned us with his deep, dark gaze. °The lives of our people depend on you. Let me explain.

°A few weeks ago a man from your world came here by accident. He had been swimming in one of your oceans wearing a metal lung. A freak storm pulled him through one of the portals that joins our worlds. He was badly hurt, so we kept him on our island and nursed him back to health. Later we learned that his name was Henry Craddock and that the lung helped him to breathe under water.°

Kallie and I looked at each other. Scuba gear, we both thought.

°He showed so much interest in us that we let him visit our city with his metal lung. We made it clear that before he returned home, we would erase all his memories of Ayralon. But he betrayed our trust. Having gained a great deal of knowledge about us, including the magic words to open the portals, he fled back to Earth before this was done. When he left, he took our most valuable possession — the sacred Jewel of Life.

°He couldn't have done anything worse, for the Jewel can never be replaced. It's the source of our magic, and it keeps our world alive. Without it we will die. Many of my people are already starting to weaken. It won't be long before all of us begin to feel the effects of this terrible loss.°

°Why did he take the jewel?° asked Kallie. °Why would he want it? Brin told me that mermagic doesn't work on Earth.°

Crispus nodded. °That's true,° he said. °But the Jewel is a rare sea-gem. It's probably worth a huge amount of money in your world. And money seems to be what Craddock is interested in. I fear we will never see the Jewel, or Henry Craddock, again.°

°Who told him about the Jewel?° Kallie asked. °I mean...how did he know where to find it?°

Crispus cleared his throat and looked uncomfortable.

Brin answered for him. °I did. We went for walks on the island beach. He was very charming. I told him all about my people and their magic. Too much. And I neglected to watch over the Jewel of Life.°

She twirled in her chair to gaze sadly at a pedestal of carved coral nearby. On it rested a large, cupped shell. The shell was empty.

°One afternoon when I was picking berries from the island garden for him, he must have slipped away and made another visit with his metal lung. He found the chamber empty. And now the Jewel is gone.°

I groaned inwardly. Henry Craddock was a thief, and in her innocence Brin had made it easy for him. I was ashamed of my human half. It was people like Craddock who made the human race look so bad. °What does the jewel look like?° I asked. °How will we know it when we see it?°

°That won't be a concern,° Crispus said, throwing an unhappy look at Brin. °I've tried to talk Brin out of this, but she won't listen. The Keeper of the Jewel will be going with you.°

Brin nodded. Her eyes blazed with anger. °This is all my fault,° she explained. °I shouldn't have trusted Henry Craddock, or told him where the Jewel was. Now my people are in danger. I must come with you and help make things right. Besides, you need me. I'm the Keeper of the Jewel, so I can sense when it is near. I can feel its magic.°

In the seconds that followed, I was thinking all this over. We'd have to find a way of explaining Brin to our family and friends. Then we'd have to act fast, for the longer she stayed on Earth, the weaker she'd become.

°I have one last question,° Kallie said. °Where does Henry Craddock live? Did he tell you what part of our world he's from?°

°He spoke of a place called Canada,° replied Crispus, °and of a city called Edmonton. Since he entered Ayralon through the same portal as you did, we believe his part of the world is close to yours. Is that true?°

°Yes, it's true,° said Kallie, °Edmonton isn't far from where we live. We'll do our best to find him. We promise.°

Then the Chief Advisor to the Ruler of Ayralon lowered his shining head in sorrow. °Thank you. You are our only hope.°

7

Tails of Magic

As we swam from the king's castle to the outer edge of the city, Kallie and I noticed that something strange was happening to our bodies.

It began with a tingling in my hands. I held them to my face and saw that tiny, golden webs had formed between my fingers and thumbs. I choked in dismay and spun back toward Kallie. To my horror I saw that her legs were ablaze with light — just as Brin's had been back at the beach. Then right before my eyes my sister's legs disappeared, and in their place gleamed the long golden tail and fins of a real mermaid.

If I'd been standing on land I'd likely have toppled over in shock. My heart thudded. The water in my lungs was suddenly too thick to breathe.

Kallie looked down, then kicked and hurtled through the water, gurgling with delight. It was clear that the mermaid tail was much more powerful than two spindly legs. What would our mother think? Was this what she had been afraid of?

A pod of nearby dolphins sensed Kallie's joy and whistled. Sharing her excitement, they sped closer and were soon leaping and dancing in circles around her. The commotion attracted some curious merchildren, followed by their mothers. I could only stare in wonder as Kallie somersaulted gleefully past my nose, dolphins and merchildren in her wake.

°I hoped this would happen,° said Brin, as Kallie and her entourage swept by. °It just took a while — with the magic in Ayralon weakened. See? It's happening to you too, Danya. But your mind is holding you back.°

I peered down at my own sparkling, tingling legs and gritted my teeth. I didn't want to let them change. I wouldn't let them change. I felt like I was being drawn deeper and deeper into a pit that I could never climb out of. I hadn't asked for this, and now even my own body was betraying me.

°Don't fight it, Danya,° advised Brin. °Like it or not, this is what you are.°

I struggled for a moment longer, then gave in, as I realized she was right.

The sensation that swept through me was somewhere between a shiver of pleasure and a throb of pain. The feeling only lasted for a few heartbeats and then it was over. I peered down, not wanting to see what I knew for certain was there. My tail.

No one had to teach me how to swim with it — I just knew. It was like going from crawling to running in one step. It was like going from pedalling a bicycle to racing a car. I skimmed. I soared. I leaped and flew. Nothing could hold me back. I was free.

When I finally came to my senses and swam back to the others, I saw that Brin had sorted everyone out and sent them away. She smiled as I cartwheeled joyfully around her, but was polite enough not to say, "I told you so." Instead she offered to take Kallie and me on a tour of the city. We eagerly agreed.

She swept us away through underwater gardens where coral blossomed like marigolds and waving plants grew as tall and thick as forests. We sailed past merfolk fishing with nets and harvesting kelp for food. We floated through the market where they traded shell bracelets and pearl necklaces for

sponges, combs and a hundred other delightful things. We drifted into the library, where books written on seaweed scrolls filled more shelves than we could count. Everywhere we went the mermaids welcomed us with soft caresses and laughter. At last Brin signalled that it was time for us to go, and when we rose to the surface, the look on Kallie's face told me how heartbroken she was to leave this world behind.

I felt sad, too, but for a different reason. Kallie's heart was completely with the merpeople now, but my own feelings were in turmoil, torn between Ayralon and Earth, between my real father and the parents I had always known. I was the true daughter of a merman — that had been proven beyond a doubt. But if I learned more about him and grew to love him, could I still be loyal to my stepfather? My mother had been afraid she would lose us to the sea, and it was already starting to happen. I no longer knew where or to whom I belonged, and it frightened me.

°Focus on making your legs reappear,° Brin told us as we swam ever closer to the surface — and the island. °Picture your body changing. Don't worry, it gets easier with practice.°

A few minutes later we were standing knee-deep in water, close to where we had first entered her world. Kallie peered longingly back at the sea. I breathed in air that felt dry and tasteless on my tongue, then reached up to squeeze the water from my hair.

"Are you ready?" asked Brin.

We both nodded, and Brin began chanting the magic words that would return us to Earth. The world spun around us, and in seconds we were floating in the pool where it had all begun. I rubbed my eyes and gazed around. Everything looked exactly the same as before.

I treaded water and took a few deep breaths. My head was whirling, not so much from the trip home, which had been quick and painless, but from everything I had been through in Ayralon.

"Look at the time," Kallie said, pointing at the clock on the wall.

I squinted up through sodden lashes. Either the clock was broken, or we had returned only minutes after we had left. I stared more closely and saw that the second hand was still moving.

"Thank goodness," I said. "This saves explaining where we've been." I glanced over at the lifeguard. "I don't think he's noticed you, Brin. He's too busy with those kids who just came in." I shook my head in confusion. "I don't understand about the time, though."

"Don't try," Brin advised. "Time just passes differently in our two worlds."

Kallie grinned. "Danya, you're too logical. Luckily I don't have that problem. I can just let it go."

"What's wrong with being logical?" I demanded.

"It limits your imagination," she said.

I started to protest, but Brin shook her head. "We have to get out of here," she said. "We don't have much time."

"You're right," I agreed, as we scrambled from the pool and headed for the change room. "The first thing we need to do is find a way to Edmonton. It's a three-hour drive. Mom and Dad will never agree to take us. And we can't just hop on a bus by ourselves!"

"I've been wondering about that, too," Kallie said. We sat Brin in a changing stall while we rinsed off in the showers. "There's only one solution — Aunt Mattie. We can tell her the truth and she'll believe us. I wouldn't be surprised if she's had some otherworld experiences of her own."

Of course — Aunt Mattie. Kallie was right. I wasn't sure I wanted to drag our aunt into this, but what choice did we have? If we ran away to Edmonton without telling our parents, it would hurt them terribly. They would send the police to track us down, and we would have to make up a story that everyone believed. Kallie and I were terrible at lying so we'd never get away with it. The more I thought about it the more complicated it got. No, Aunt Mattie was the only answer.

We wrapped a wet towel around Brin's sparkling legs, and she and I hurried home, pushing my bike. Kallie rode on ahead and kept Mom busy in the kitchen so I could sneak Brin up to my room and find something for her to wear.

A few minutes later I was introducing her to Mom as a new friend of ours.

Mom returned Brin's bright smile and held out a plate of cookies. "Are you helping out with the planting?" she asked. So far so good. It looked like it was going to be one of those times when she didn't ask a lot of questions.

Later that afternoon, after we had planted every pea and radish and lettuce seed in the garden, we hurried over to Aunt Mattie's house and banged on her front door. She didn't seem at all surprised to see us. Smiling at Brin, she invited us in with a flutter of her jewelled hand.

"I've been expecting you," she said, closing the door quickly behind us. Perfume hovered around her like drifting petals. As the three of us trailed behind her into the kitchen, her bracelets tinkled and her long skirt brushed the floor. I wondered how she kept from tripping on the hem. She pulled out some chairs and we all sat down at the table.

Aunt Mattie studied us thoughtfully through impossibly lush and long eyelashes. "There's a problem with the Balance of Magic," she said. "Is that why you're here?"

"No," I said.

"Yes," replied Kallie. "At least I think so. I'm not sure if the problem you're talking about is the same as ours, though."

"I knew it," Aunt Mattie clucked with satisfaction. "It's been a nightmare. There's magic everywhere there shouldn't be and none where it's supposed to be. You can't imagine how hard it is on the nerves. What's your problem, dears? Why did you bring a mermaid with you? Is there some misplaced magic that you need me to help you find?"

I just stared at her with my mouth hanging open.

"Yes," said Brin. "It came from Ayralon."

Aunt Mattie nodded. "Of course," she said. "The magic in Ayralon is very powerful. But it won't work in our world. Most magic doesn't, and most people don't believe in it anyway." She was too polite to look at me, but her words hung in the air between us. She didn't need to remind me that until a few hours ago I was one of those people.

"The human who stole it doesn't care about the magic," said Brin. "He's just interested in getting rich."

"Of course he is," said Aunt Mattie. "That's how humans are trained to think. So your villain is greedy, but he's not stupid if he's made it this far. Tell me," she continued, "what does the magic look like? It must have a physical form."

"It's a large and beautiful jewel," Kallie said.

My mouth was still hanging open but I couldn't seem to close it. Yesterday Aunt Mattie seemed like the nuttiest person I knew. Now she sounded like the wisest human being on the planet. Suddenly I wanted to apologize for what I had thought over the years. "Aunt Mattie..." I began, but she just shook her head.

"Don't worry about that now, dear."

"Have you ever been to Ayralon, Aunt Mattie?" Kallie asked.

Aunt Mattie smiled and wagged a scarlet-tipped finger. "That's my secret. But I do know that your real father was from Ayralon, and that the two of you were born there."

"If you knew about our real father, why didn't you

tell us?" demanded Kallie, looking insulted.

"It wasn't my secret to tell," she explained. "But that wasn't the only problem. Kallie, you might have believed me, but Danya wouldn't have. And it would have made things more awkward between us."

She was right, of course. I hung my head as she studied me thoughtfully. "Is something the matter, Danya?" she asked. "That's a pretty long face you're wearing."

I hesitated, not knowing how to explain.

"I know what's wrong," said Brin softly. She turned to me. "Danya, you think if you believe in your merfather and Ayralon, it's like rejecting your parents. Especially your stepfather. Is that true?"

Though I shook my head, I had to admit that it was. Brin had explained my feelings when I couldn't myself.

"Danya, I know this hasn't been easy," interrupted Kallie, "but right now we need to make a plan. How are we going to get to Edmonton? Aunt Mattie, that's where the thief — Henry Craddock — lives."

"Oh, that's easy," I said, relieved that we weren't talking about my feelings anymore. "Aunt Mattie can drive us."

Brin shivered. She had seen more than enough of driving on the walk over. "Are you sure that's the only way?" she asked unhappily.

Aunt Mattie nodded. "Here's what I think we should do," she said. "I'll ask your parents if I can take the three of you for the rest of the weekend. And before we set out, I'll learn all I can about this Henry Craddock." She paused and winked at me. "Don't look so doubtful, Danya. I'm a woman of many talents. Monday is a school holiday, but businesses are still open. That will give us two full days. I'll find out where Mr. Craddock works, and maybe even where he lives. Don't worry, my dears. We'll get the jewel back."

I smiled back at her and tried to look like I believed her. I was probably being too logical again, but I was seriously worried. Aunt Mattie's car could hardly make it to the end of the street, let alone all the way to Edmonton. And once we got there — if we got there — what would we do? Would we just march into his office and demand the Jewel of Life? The kind of man who would steal it in the first place was also the kind of man who wouldn't give it up without a fight. And then there was the problem of Brin. How long would her strength hold out?

I groaned to myself. What had we gotten ourselves into?

"Don't fret, dear," cooed Aunt Mattie, patting my

hand. "These things have a way of working out in the end."

But it was what might happen before the end that had me worried.

8

To the Rescue

We spent the night at Aunt Mattie's, and Sunday afternoon we all climbed into her battered old car and headed north to Edmonton. In spite of my misgivings, the day couldn't have been lovelier. The sun blazed in a sky as clear as crystal. The heavy cloak of winter was almost gone, replaced with the brighter attire of green grass and budding flowers. The air, though still cool on our skin, held the promise of warmer days to come.

We stopped in Red Deer for gas and climbed out of the car to stretch our legs. I kept my fingers crossed, and sighed in relief when Aunt Mattie started it up again and the poor wreck sputtered to life.

"I don't know why you're so worried," Aunt Mattie said, as we clattered back onto the highway. "This is a good car."

"I believe you," said Brin innocently.

I looked at Kallie and rolled my eyes. Aunt Mattie saw me in the mirror and pretended to be insulted. "That's the trouble with young people these days," she said, patting the dash lovingly. "You don't recognize quality when you see it." We all had a good laugh, then went on to talk about some of the places we thought Brin might like to visit, like Disneyland (Kallie's pick) and the Calgary Stampede (mine). Eventually our lighthearted chatter turned to more serious matters.

"During my research, I learned that Henry Craddock is an engineer," our aunt explained, her face suddenly grim. "He runs an oil company."

"Engineers make lots of money," I said. "So why did he steal the Jewel?"

"Some people — no matter how much they have — always want more," said Kallie.

Aunt Mattie nodded in agreement. "His business might be in trouble," she said. "Sometimes people make mistakes and end up owing money they can't pay back. Maybe he just got in over his head."

We sat in silence for a while, lost in thought. Didn't Henry Craddock realize that by taking the Jewel of Life, he had placed the Ayralonians in great danger? Perhaps he didn't care, but I hoped he wasn't as hard-hearted as that.

"I don't think he knew," said Brin in answer to my unspoken question. "I'm sure he didn't mean to hurt us."

"Maybe not, but the result's still the same," said Kallie grimly.

We reached Edmonton just before suppertime and searched for a restaurant to soothe our growling stomachs. We could order whatever we wanted as long as the meal included fresh vegetables, protein and not too much fat. When you're with Aunt Mattie, you might as well forget about hamburgers and french fries. Fast food goes against everything she stands for. In spite of that, we managed to convince her to let Brin try "burgersinfrize" — with extra lettuce and tomatoes.

Afterwards Aunt Mattie found a motel nearby, and rented a room with two double beds and free videos. We agreed to watch only one, so we could get off to an early start tracking down Henry Craddock. But we forgot that Brin had never seen a movie before. After the second one Aunt Mattie had to unplug the TV and hide the remote so Brin would go to sleep.

First thing Monday morning we headed downtown with Aunt Mattie at the wheel.

After circling a few blocks she found the building where Henry Craddock worked, and parked the car nearby. Then we stood together in the lobby for a moment, gathering our courage. It was one thing to come up with a plan while sitting in Aunt Mattie's bright, safe kitchen, and quite another to walk open-eyed into the lion's den. But we hadn't come all this way to turn back now. Agreeing that Brin should stay out of sight until we saw how Craddock reacted, we took a few deep breaths and marched toward the elevator.

Craddock's offices were only three floors up, and they looked so harmless and ordinary that I almost laughed in relief. A large oak desk faced the doorway in the reception area. Silk plants brightened up the corners and paintings of prairie sunsets decorated the walls. Behind the desk was a closed door with Henry Craddock's name on it. To the left was a hallway that led to more offices and supply rooms. Somewhere here the precious Jewel of Life could be hidden. I looked over at Brin and could tell by the excitement in her eyes that my guess was right. Then she slipped

behind a large tropical plant while the rest of us paused in front of the desk.

Craddock's receptionist looked up from her computer screen and smiled, and everything ordinary about the room vanished.

"Hello," she said, rising to her feet. "My name is Hali. May I help you?"

We saw a beautiful creature, her hair so white that it gleamed like snow in sunlight. Cut short, it hugged her head like a silky cap, framing a wide brow and delicate chin. Blue eyes engulfed us, so dark they seemed almost purple. Her pale green dress seemed to float about her slender form like feathers, and her voice sang like bells and harp strings in our ears.

We all stood and gawked at her, too surprised to speak. She was so strange and lovely, yet I noticed there were dark smudges under her eyes.

Aunt Mattie was the first to recover. "Have we met before?" she asked.

The girl shook her head. "I'm sure we haven't. How may I help you?"

"We've come to see Mr. Craddock," Kallie said.

"May I tell him your names?"

"We want to surprise him."

Hali nodded and turned away. She picked up the phone, pressed some numbers, and asked Mr.

Craddock if she could send some visitors in to see him. I wondered what he would say when we told him what we wanted. If he refused to talk to us, what would we do? I didn't have long to fret, for a moment later Hali hung up the phone and told us to go through.

9

The Escape

I had expected Henry Craddock to look like a greasy-haired, shifty-eyed villain — not the handsome, clean-cut individual who answered our knock. Ash blond hair curled gently about his ears. Large brown eyes peered at us with an innocence I almost believed was real. When he smiled, dimples creased his cheeks and charm oozed from every pore. He was smiling now.

"You're not the clients I was expecting," he said in a deep, melodious voice. "But since you're here, what can I do for you?"

He made a pretty picture, but that didn't fool us.

Aunt Mattie held back, giving Kallie and I the chance to speak. I just shook my head, made a few squeaking sounds, and hoped Kallie would take over. My sister studied Craddock for a second, then chose her words with care.

"We've been sent here by some friends — to bring back something you borrowed," she said. I was surprised at how calm and cool she sounded.

He nodded thoughtfully as he closed the door behind us. "And what did your friends say I borrowed?" he asked. I couldn't be sure, but it seemed to me that his face paled slightly. Or it could have been a trick of the light.

"A magic jewel," said Kallie, and smiled sweetly.

"Aah," he responded. "And who are these friends of yours?" There was a distinct chill in his voice.

"They're from a place called Ayralon," Kallie said. "I heard you just got back from there." She didn't mention mermaids or underwater cities. Neither did he.

"Where did you get the idea that I've been to such a place?" he asked. "Perhaps you have me confused with someone else."

"I don't have you confused with anyone," said my sister in a mild voice. "Our friends knew you quite well. You spent several weeks with them, I believe."

"I don't have to listen to this," Henry Craddock said coldly, yanking open the door. "You've made a mistake. Please leave."

Kallie shook her head. "No, we haven't made a mistake." Then she let the bomb drop. "You stole the Jewel of Life from the Ayralonians. Without it, they will die. Is that how you're going to repay them for saving your life?"

"I don't know what you're talking about," Henry Craddock said.

"Oh, but I think you do," Kallie said.

Then Brin stepped through the open doorway and into the room.

When Craddock saw her, he turned pale and clenched the doorknob so hard that his knuckles whitened. He glanced in alarm at a briefcase that was lying on his desk, then back at Brin. It took me a moment to realize what this meant. Brin, who must have sensed the magic as soon as she entered the room, darted forward and threw open the lid.

We stood in stunned amazement as a rainbow of colour burst out, spilling light like spinning diamonds over everything in the room. Magic sprayed over us, cool and clean as water. Slamming the briefcase shut again, Brin grabbed it by the handle and turned to run.

Craddock lunged, knocking her off balance. The briefcase flew from her hand and landed with a thud at my feet. Craddock whirled to retrieve it, but Kallie stuck out her foot and sent him crashing to the floor. Grabbing the handle, I bolted past Hali, ignoring her shocked stare, and headed for the hallway. Brin and Kallie pounded at my heels. I didn't take the time to look back, but I heard Craddock yell at Aunt Mattie to get out of his way. Good for her. She was trying to buy us as much time as she could.

Not wanting to wait for an elevator, we shot past to the stairs. I could hear Craddock pelting along the hallway behind us. Down the stairway we thudded, bursting into the main lobby and jostling a clump of startled office workers, then out onto the street.

"Run to the car!" Aunt Mattie shrieked behind us. She clung to Craddock's sleeve, her jaw clenched in determination. Jerking his arm in an effort to shake her loose, he dragged her across the sidewalk after us. We dived for the car doors just as he caught up with us. I yanked on the nearest handle. Locked. Craddock lunged, and I felt an iron arm circle my neck while his other arm, dragging Aunt Mattie, groped for the case. With my last ounce of strength I flung it high into the air and over the car, to Kallie on the other side.

She did her best to catch it, but fear had increased my strength. The briefcase sailed over her head and halfway across the street, where it crashed to the ground with a heavy splat. We froze in horror as it exploded open, sending a shower of documents and the jewel directly into the path of an oncoming gravel truck.

Craddock shoved me roughly aside. I fell to my knees with a whimper of pain. The truck thundered past, spewing dust and fumes into our faces. I saw the papers flutter around its enormous wheels like a cloud of helpless butterflies. Then it was gone, leaving behind the remains of Craddock's briefcase and its contents.

The light at the corner turned red, giving us time to run out and assess the damage. Craddock got there first. He stared at the mess on the road, gave his mangled case a vicious kick and turned away, his face dark with rage. Then Aunt Mattie took a look and her face whitened. Kallie burst into tears.

I was the last to see. Pain swelled in my throat, making it hard to swallow. I fell to my knees beside a small pile of rainbow dust that lay glittering in the sunlight. A sudden gust of wind whirled most of it away, revealing one small fragment the size of a dime. I picked it up and held it gently between my fingers.

As I watched, a tiny light flickered deep inside of it, then went out.

I looked up to see Brin teetering weakly on her feet as her magic began to drain away.

10

Return to Ayralon

"This is all your fault," Craddock growled. "If you hadn't interfered, we'd still have the jewel."

We had returned to the sidewalk. Brin, weakened by the loss of the jewel's magic, was propped up between Aunt Mattie and Kallie. Cars whizzed up and down the street in front of us. I had slipped what was left of the jewel into my jeans pocket. The rest had been scattered by the wind, or dusted the tires of cars long gone.

My sister and Craddock exchanged glares. "You would still have it, you mean," she said.

Craddock ignored her, but his next words came

out as though he had spit them. "Be sure and tell your fishy friends that you're the ones who destroyed their precious Jewel of Life. This is your fault, not mine." He turned and stomped back into the building. If the door hadn't been automatic, he'd have slammed it. I caught a glimpse of Hali's worried, wide-eyed face pressed against the lobby window. Then she, too, was gone.

Anger blazed in Kallie's eyes. She started after him but I held her back with my hand.

"Forget him," I said to her. "It's not worth it. Nothing you say to him will change anything." My stomach felt cold and heavy, like I had swallowed a stone. I couldn't remember when I'd ever felt so terrible. And I was sure Kallie was feeling ten times worse. How could we return to Ayralon and face Brin's people with such a sorry tale? But we had to get back, and quickly. We had to let Crispus know what had happened, in case there was something he could do. Perhaps he and the other advisors could think of another way to help Brin save the merpeople.

"We need water," Kallie mumbled, and started to cry. She wasn't talking about finding something to drink, either. We loaded Brin into the car and scrambled in after. Aunt Mattie handed Kallie a

Kleenex, then took out a city map and unfolded it in front of us.

"Look at this," she said, tracing a route with her finger. "If we take Stony Plain Road over to here and then head south, we'll end up at West Edmonton Mall. There's a pool there. Will that help?" Then without waiting for an answer, she started the engine and roared out onto the street.

Every kid in Alberta has heard of the pool at West Edmonton Mall. It has twenty-two water slides. Or is it twenty-three? Our parents had taken us there several times, and we had always loved it. Right now we were both too miserable to care.

In less than an hour we were standing inside the mall, with Brin braced on wobbly legs between us. Aunt Mattie shoved some money into our hands so we could pay the entrance fee and kissed us goodbye. "I'll wait for you here," she told us. "Good luck." We started to turn away.

"Just a minute," she called out to us. "That receptionist of Craddock's — something about her made me feel tingly all over. And I've heard that name before...Hali. It's an old Greek name. It means 'the sea.' But it's probably nothing," she added, waving us away. "You better go."

We changed quickly into our bathing suits and

helped Brin peel off her clothes. I noticed with alarm that she was becoming too weak to hold her human shape. Quickly we bundled her in a towel and pulled her into the pool, towel and all.

I squeezed my hand shut over the tiny piece of jewel, pressing it deep into my palm. I whispered the magic words along with Kallie, then closed my eyes as the funnel of water rose up around us, carrying us back to Ayralon.

No mermaids came to greet us as we splashed up on the empty shore. Brin lay in the shallows, too spent even to lift her tail.

"Go without me," she whispered. "I'll be safe here. Take the broken jewel to Crispus."

Kallie and I wasted no more time. We stared at each other in wordless fear at what we might soon find, then plunged into the sea. As we sank deep beneath the waves, our lungs filled with water and we breathed easily enough. But our legs remained, and no webs formed between our fingers. The magic was too far gone for that.

We swam until the city of Kahului spread out before us, still breathtaking, but darker, and strangely still. We glided through the empty streets with only the fishes for company. Peering in a doorway, we saw a sleeping mermaid held in place by the cords of her seaweed bed. House after house revealed the same sad sight until we realized, with sick despair, that this was a sleep from which the merpeople might never wake.

At last we entered Brin's conference chamber. No guards drifted forward to greet us. No curious eyes turned our way. The sleep of death hung over all the merfolk as we threaded our way among the drifting bodies.

We paused in front of the hanging chairs. I stared at Crispus's lifeless form, my hands clenched so tightly that the jewel fragment bit into my palm. But that small prick of pain was nothing compared to the sorrow in my heart. Alora lay at his side, her hair floating about her shoulders like a silk-spun cloud. One hand stretched toward him in a silent gesture for help.

Tears filled my eyes, melting into the water around me. I glanced at Kallie and saw her blink away tears of her own.

°Don't cry, dear children,° came a weak, watery voice. °You did the best you could. It was a difficult thing we asked of you. No one is to blame.°

Crispus's dark eyes peered sadly at us. One hand feebly beckoned. We drifted closer.

°We have bad news about the Jewel of Life,° I

began, reaching out my hand to show the tiny fragment I still carried.

He nodded. °We know,° he whispered. °We felt it break.° His eyes fell shut, as if speaking had taken all his strength. Kallie and I kicked forward in alarm, fearing the worst. Then his eyelids fluttered open again.

°Oh, don't give up!° my sister exclaimed. °We'll do whatever it takes to save Ayralon! Where did the jewel come from? We can find another one!°

°I'm sorry, Kallie,° he said. °It has been part of the magic of our world for centuries. And it cannot be replaced.°

°Are you sure?° Kallie cried.

Alora stirred. °Chief Advisor, that's not entirely true...° she whispered. °There are the sea nymphs...°

°But it's been so long,° Crispus murmured. °We haven't seen them for more years than I can count.°

°It is said,° Alora explained, °that sea nymphs live far below, deep in the oceans of Ayralon, in a crystal cave. They have great magic. Hundreds of years ago they gave the Jewel of Life to us. They care about the merpeople and want us to be happy...°

°I'm afraid the nymphs are gone now,° Crispus said. °When Henry Craddock took the jewel, I sent merdivers to find the crystal cave and ask for help.

The divers came back and reported that the cave was empty.°

Kallie wasn't ready to give up. °Please tell us where the crystal cave is,° she said. °We want to look for ourselves. Please.°

The Chief Advisor shook his head. His eyes had clouded over, and it seemed as though he would soon disappear behind them, never to return.

°The dolphins,° he whispered. °The dolphins will take you anywhere you want to go. All you have to do is ask...° His voice trailed off into silence. This time his eyes didn't open again.

11

The Dolphins

The dolphins came to us only a few minutes after we called. More than the urgency in our voices had brought them, for their sad eyes told us they knew exactly what we needed.

As one of them nudged against me, the feeling of affection that surged up inside of me when I touched her smooth, silky skin filled me with surprise. And somehow I knew instantly that her name was Storm-At-Sea, that she was a fast swimmer and proud of it, and that she loved the merfolk very much.

Kallie had always been crazy for dolphins. She would bring home stacks of dolphin books and gobble them up like novels. I used to laugh at her and remind her that there were no dolphins on the prairie. Studying about them, in my opinion, was a waste of time.

I wasn't laughing now.

I still remembered her excitement when she told me what she had learned.

"They can stay under water for fifteen minutes without breathing," she had said. "They're mammals, you know. They eat all kinds of things, and they use echolocation to find their food — and did you know they swallow it whole? They can talk with clicks, whistles and groans. They can swim fifty-five kilometres an hour and leap six metres in the air!"

Thanks to my sister, I figured I was close to being an expert on dolphins.

I got a grip on Storm-At-Sea's slippery dorsal fin and we launched out. Kallie was close behind, clinging to a dolphin named Wind-Over-Waves. She was smiling, enjoying the ride in spite of everything. I was just hoping Storm-At-Sea wasn't planning any six-metre dolphin leaps at breakneck speed.

The next moment a little tickle of thought inside my head assured me that she wasn't. I was so surprised that I nearly let go. As far as I knew, the dolphins in my world didn't talk to people in their heads. At least, Kallie had never mentioned it. I couldn't help but wonder if my sister was having the same thought-sharing experience with Wind-Over-Waves. Judging by the look of concentration on her face, I guessed that she was.

The pod of dolphins swam for a long time. Farther and farther out to sea they took us, where there was only the rolling ocean and the great blue sky overhead. Then they slowed, circled in the water and whistled to each other in their own musical language. I sensed them agree on the place, and felt them prompt us to hang on tightly.

Then they dived.

Down they carried us to where the sea darkened and grew cold and even the bravest fishes dared not follow. At those depths, the pressure mounted rapidly. Every breath was agony. I felt wrapped in a blanket of cold that grew thicker and heavier as we descended. I could no longer speak. Images grew muddled in my head. My dolphin sent little thought-bubbles of encouragement into my mind, but I could sense her growing anxiety. Farther and farther we fell into the frigid blackness, until I knew I would never make it to the cave alive. But I was too numb to care.

If I had opened my eyes I would have noticed the light sooner. But it wasn't until Storm-At-Sea halted and I bumped against her that I realized something was happening. I forced myself to look.

The light spilled from a crack in a jagged cliff face that rose up from the ocean floor like a huge black wall. The dolphins nudged our limp bodies toward the opening. An invisible barrier of some kind resisted, then gave way. We tumbled helplessly, caught in a warm current of water that sucked us closer and closer to the source of light. Behind us, the dolphins clicked and whistled goodbye. We sensed rather than saw them turn away and speed upward toward the surface.

As the warm water flowed over us it gradually thawed our aching limbs. Breathing grew easier, and when our thoughts cleared, we gazed at each other in dazed relief, happy to be alive. We drifted through a passageway that carried us along faster and faster until it suddenly pushed us out into a huge, underwater cave.

A glittering network of crystals encircled us — white, pink, pale blue and green — so delicate that I feared one wrong move would send them swirling down around us. We stared at them, too awestruck to speak. They were like clouds in a summer sky — the closer we looked, the more wonders we discovered.

We saw tiny forests, and snowflakes, and fairy

castles that sat amid gardens of flowers. Strings of lace looped like curtains, and cobwebs glistened, pebbled with drops of dew. The light that filled the cave seemed to come from everywhere and all around us, as if each crystal burned with a deep, inner fire.

°It's awesome,° said Kallie. °I could look at this all day. But we need to find the sea nymphs. Do you see anything?°

I twirled slowly in the water, searching.

°No, nothing. Maybe they're hiding nearby. Or maybe they're invisible,° I said hopefully.

°Let's explain to them why we're here and show them the broken jewel,° Kallie suggested. °Maybe they'll notice us. Should I go first?°

°Go ahead,° I said. °We have nothing to lose.° I held up the fragment of the Jewel of Life.

Kallie gazed around the cave one last time, then turned toward me. I nodded in encouragement. She began.

°Nymphs of Ayralon, we're here because we need your help. Our people — that is, the merfolk of Ayralon — are very sick. Do you remember the jewel you gave them a long time ago? Well, it's broken. You probably already know this, but without it the mermaids will die. Please help us find another one before it's too late.°

We gazed around and waited, but nothing moved. We waited longer. I decided it was my turn to try. If we couldn't get their attention, all was lost. As I opened my mouth to speak, the fragment of jewel floated up from my palm and away, caught in a small eddy of water.

°Do you see that piece of jewel?° I asked the invisible beings. °It's all that's left of the Jewel of Life. I realize you created it and you're probably upset, but please don't blame the merfolk. If you want to punish someone, then punish me. I threw the briefcase too far, and Kallie couldn't catch it.°

Sorrow swelled inside of me. I could hear the hysteria in my voice. I felt the prickle of tears in my eyes, but I no longer cared.

°It landed in the middle of the road,° I continued with a sob. °And then a gravel truck ran over it. Now they're going to die, and it's all my fault.°

I closed my eyes and felt the tears squeeze out between my lids. I waited for something to happen, but when I opened them again there was only the empty cave and a silence that seemed to last forever.

The Crystal Cave

Kallie and I watched the fragment of jewel spin toward the centre of the cave. In a few minutes it would be carried out of sight and lost forever. But what did it matter now? This one small piece wasn't enough to save the merfolk, anyway. I hung motionless in the water beside Kallie, my heart breaking to pieces inside me.

°It's okay, Danya,° she said. °You did your best.°

I shook my head to tell her that it wasn't okay, that nothing was okay or ever would be again. But before I could speak, something blinked into existence right under my nose. One moment we were alone, and the next we were surrounded by dozens of tiny creatures that darted and flitted past us so quickly that our eyes could hardly follow them. At first they looked like fish, with bodies made of diamonds and orange flame for eyes. Then they were fairies that spun in circles through the water, trailing rainbow bubbles from their wings. Then they were both, and neither. They flickered around us like a dazzle of sparks above a fire. We stared at the amazing sight, too enthralled to speak. At last one of them broke away from the group and glided toward us.

It hovered above us for a moment. Then the tiny, glittery parts of its body swirled more fiercely and drew together to form a solid being.

She was an exquisite little creature. Her body looked like moonlight glistening on silk and her wings were sheer and gauzy. Kallie and I gawked at her, but she didn't seem to mind. She just smiled, then reached out a tiny hand to scoop up the broken jewel as it floated by.

Light exploded all around us. I closed my eyes against the glare, then covered my face with my hands, peeking out between my fingers.

The sea nymph's strange and beautiful face was framed with silver hair. Streamers of the palest green floated around her, and she studied us with eyes bluer than the clearest, deepest sea.

°Hali!° we both cried.

It was indeed Henry Craddock's receptionist — but not as we had seen her on Earth. This miniature, winged Hali glowed with life and energy.

°This is my true form,° she explained while we stared. °I'm sorry there was no one here in the cave to meet you. We didn't know you were coming. This is only one of the many places we live.°

°That's all right,° we squeaked.

°I must explain,° she continued. °As you already know, we are the sea nymphs. When life began in Ayralon, the sea nymphs and the merfolk shared the magic of this world equally. But as the centuries passed, the Balance of Magic gradually became more and more lopsided.°

(Balance of Magic? Another point for Aunt Mattie.)

°Because of this upset in the Balance, the merfolk lost their magic. They grew weaker and weaker. We finally realized that they couldn't live without it, and soon they would all be gone. We knew something had to be done to save them, so we created the Jewel of Life to replace the magic they had lost. Ever since that time, we've made it our duty to watch over and protect them.

°We don't reveal ourselves often — they are strong and independent, and we want them to stay that way. But when we learned that the jewel was stolen and taken to your world, we were greatly alarmed, for we knew the mermaids wouldn't survive long without it.°

°Couldn't you make another one?° asked Kallie.

°Alas, we did not remember how. Those who created it are gone,° Hali explained. °We could have figured it out in time — but time was the one thing we didn't have. So I went to Earth to find the jewel, not realizing how weak I would become in a world without our magic. I posed as a human and convinced Henry Craddock to hire me as temporary office help. There I was in your world, drained of strength, nearly drained of magic, hardly able to hold my human shape. I could feel the jewel's magic nearby, but it is a different magic from my own, so I couldn't find it, or use it to renew my strength.

°When you came, I was overjoyed. Then the jewel was crushed — and I feared all was lost. But, Danya, I saw you slip the broken piece into your pocket and I knew that we were saved, for here in Ayralon we have the power to make the jewel whole again. It's like kindling a fire from a live coal. All we need is a piece.°

Hali held out her tiny hand.

Kallie and I hung motionless as the jewel fragment flickered, then throbbed and swelled. Unable to speak, we watched it grow brighter and larger. We stared as it whirled and glittered in front of us, scattering sparks of light that drenched our skin in magic.

Suspended above Hali's palm blazed an enormous gem — whole and round and perfect.

I breathed in the magic and willed my clumsy legs to disappear. A sudden, throbbing ache surged through my body. My mermaid tail shimmered into existence. Kallie laughed beside me as her own tail appeared. It took all of my willpower not to whirl around the cave in sheer ecstasy.

Hali's lovely eyes sparkled with amusement as she watched us. It was as though she knew us better than we knew ourselves. °Take the Jewel of Life,° she said to Kallie, who was nearest. °Thank you for everything you have done. It's strange, there's a song my people sing that tells of children from another world who will heal that which is broken. I wonder...°

Then with a flash of light and the sound of tinkling bells, she was gone.

I looked at Kallie. Kallie looked at me. I shrugged my shoulders.

°Go ahead,° I told her. °I brought the jewel here. It's your turn now.°

The smile on her face was all the thanks I needed. As she cradled it in her palm, her face glowed in its glittering, rainbow light. But it was the happiness in her eyes that shone more brightly.

We left the warmth and beauty of the cave behind and drifted out into the passageway. I prepared to struggle against the swiftly moving current that had carried us inside, but the moment we entered the tunnel, the water magically changed direction. Without effort we tumbled back the way we had come and out into the sea.

This time the jewel lit our journey, though the icy water still sapped the strength from our aching muscles. We had hardly begun to rise when a cluster of dark forms swooped toward us. Two familiar faces grinned at us from the darkness.

°Storm-At-Sea and Wind-Over-Waves are back!° I exclaimed as the dolphins bumped joyfully against us.

Kallie hesitated, one arm thrown over her dolphin's back. °This isn't right,° she said, placing the jewel in my hand. °You're the one who saved it. You're the one who should take it back. That's just how it's supposed to be.°

°Are you sure?°

°I'm totally sure.°

I paused, then reached out and touched her hand. °Thanks, Kallie,° I said.

We hurtled upwards through layers of water that gradually grew warmer and brighter until once again we were skimming across the surface of the ocean. We travelled beneath the sun in a blissful dream, with only the gulls for company. Closer and closer to the island — and Brin.

And there she was, gliding happily toward us — her arms outstretched and her hair streaming. The healing magic of the Jewel of Life had reached her.

We circled back, the lead dolphin carrying the Ruler of Ayralon, heading for Kahului. The journey gave me a chance to think over everything that had happened. During the last few hours, something inside of me had changed. I felt like I belonged in Ayralon now. It had become part of me, like breathing underwater and talking to dolphins and discovering magic deep beneath the sea.

Of course you belong, said a tickle of thought inside my head. *You were born here.*

°But I love Earth, too,° I said.

Yes, agreed my dolphin. *It's your home.*

°How can that be? I feel love for my real father,

though I've never met him, but I love my stepfather, too. If my mother knew, what would she say? If my stepfather found out, how would he feel?°

He would be happy for you, said Storm-At-Sea, *because that's the way love is.*

Down, down we dove to the outskirts of the mer-city, where we parted with our dolphin friends. They spiralled away above us, whistling in farewell.

As we swam through the darkened streets, magic spilled from the jewel in my hand and seeped into every corner and crevice of the city. All around us the merfolk woke from their death-like sleep, stretched and gazed around in surprise. Many waved when they saw us and glided near. We greeted them with hugs of joy.

Brin held our hands and swam between us to the centre of the city and the Ruler's Hall, where her advisors waited. As we made our way along the passageway, the lamps on the walls flickered to life above us, and the merfolk bowed to let us pass. Brin swirled into the hanging chair next to a beaming Crispus, and I gently placed the Jewel of Life in its place of honour on the pedestal.

°As Keeper of the Jewel, and Ruler of Ayralon,° Brin announced, °I thank you, Leron's children, on behalf of all the merfolk.° Then she added, °Welcome home, Kallie and Danya!° and a great roar went up from the crowd.

For the first time, I felt I had truly come home.

The next few days slipped blissfully by, but finally the time came for us to leave Ayralon and head back to Earth — our other home. Aunt Mattie was still waiting beside the pool in West Edmonton Mall, and we weren't sure how much Earth time had passed. Here we were in Ayralon having the time of our lives, while she still didn't know how things had turned out or what had become of us.

Our last minutes were spent at the Hall, saying goodbye to Brin.

°Please come back and visit as often as you can,° she said, kissing us both on the cheek.

°Just try and keep us away!° Kallie laughed.

We turned to Crispus. His dark eyes studied us thoughtfully. °Before you go, there's something I want to tell you,° he said.

°What's that?° we asked him.

°I've never seen such joy on a child's face,° he said. °In the beginning, all I saw in you was sadness and confusion. But when you brought the jewel back to us, your face was like the sun above the sea.°

°Whose face?° I asked. °Do you mean Kallie's?°
He shook his head. °No. Yours,° he said.

*E*pilogue

"*I*'m so proud of you, Danya," my stepfather said.

I was curled up on the couch beside him. I had just pulled my language arts assignment from my binder and thrust it under his nose. Half-blind though he was, he couldn't miss the huge "A" that was scrawled in red at the top of the page.

The mythological creatures I had chosen to write about were (of course) mermaids. The truth of the matter was, they weren't as mythological as everyone thought. But that was a secret I didn't plan on spilling any time soon.

"I knew you could do it," my stepfather said, kissing me on the cheek.

A few seconds later Mom, Kallie and Aunt Mattie burst into the room. Mom was toting a huge bowl of popcorn so warm and buttery it made my mouth water. Kallie had the video. Aunt Mattie was balancing a stack of glasses in one hand and a pitcher of orange juice in the other. When everything was set on the coffee table, Dad flicked on the TV and Kallie started the movie.

I sighed in contentment and rested my head against Dad's shoulder. It felt so wonderful for us all to be together like this. I peeked past his stubbly chin and grinned at Kallie. She smiled back. We were still as different as twins could be — but in the last few days we had shared a magic world together. It was hard to believe. I looked at Aunt Mattie. She jiggled her bracelets and winked.

Vicki Blum lives in High River, Alberta, where she enjoys going for long walks and looking at the mountains. As an elementary-school librarian, she loves working with books and doing workshops with young writers. The five books in her best-selling series — *Wish Upon a Unicorn, The Shadow Unicorn, The Land Without Unicorns, The Promise of the Unicorn* and *A Gathering of Unicorns* — have enchanted thousands of young readers.

Also by Vicki Blum: The Unicorn Collection

Wish Upon a Unicorn
by Vicki Blum

Arica falls through a crack in her grandmother's floor — and into Bundelag, a world of fairies, trolls, elves and unicorns, where the unicorns need her help.

ISBN 0-590-51519-5

Book One in the Unicorn Collection

The Shadow Unicorn
by Vicki Blum

Arica returns to the magical land of Bundelag to find that evil Raden — helped by the Shadow unicorn — has turned the other unicorns to stone. All but one . . .

ISBN 0-439-98706-7

Book Two in the Unicorn Collection

The Land Without Unicorns
by Vicki Blum

The precious *Book of Fairies* must be retrieved from the dangerous lands of South Bundelag. Can Arica trust the Shadow unicorn to help her?

ISBN 0-439-98863-2

Book Three in the Unicorn Collection

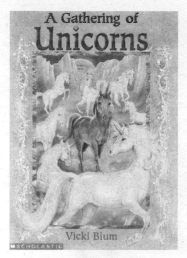

The Promise of the Unicorn

by Vicki Blum

Raden has poisoned Arica's mother. Arica must brave Dragon Island to find the rainbow flower that can save her.

ISBN 0-439-98967-1

Book Four in the Unicorn Collection

A Gathering of Unicorns

by Vicki Blum

Even with Arica's help, can the magical creatures of North Bundelag defend themselves against invaders from the South?

ISBN 0-439-97417-8

Book Five in the Unicorn Collection